UNINTENDED REBEL

LANCE ERLICK

Finlee Augare Books (Chicago)

Finlee Augare Books, Chicago, IL
ISBN: 978-1-943080-13-7 (print)
ISBN: 978-1-943080-14-4 (e-book)

Printed in the United States of America

Sometimes life takes an unexpected turn

ONE

I studied the black-haired Chinese boy on the roof of Michael's School for Boys. The private concrete institution stood diagonally across the street from my public high school with bars on the windows, razor wire all around, and security patrols dressed in black mechanical exoskeletons despite the heat.

"How did you end up behind barbed wire?" I whispered under my breath, wishing my words could reach him. "By the way, I'm Annabelle Scott, a junior. My mom's a state senator, in the political opposition; and I could get prison just for watching you." Yet I couldn't pull away.

I'd been observing the orange-uniformed boy for weeks, trying to get up the courage to do something. But what? I jumped like a paranoid squirrel at the slightest noise: the wind brushing against nearby solar panels. Or was that one of the wind generators shifting direction.

"Why does our glorious Federal Union lock you boys away?" A rhetorical question I was forbidden to ask. "Are you a dangerous brute as my Cabbage-faced Civics teacher says? Would you hurt me given a chance?"

Another white flash came from his direction.

"Are you signaling me?"

I wanted to talk with this other to find out if we had anything in common. I couldn't use e-com; our beloved Federal Union tracked every wave. They probably had eyes watching me even then. Separating the boy from me was a busy street filled with bicycles and buses. There were no personal motorized vehicles, which the city of Knoxville had banned to encourage the use of buses and bikes. Next to the boy's institution and directly across from me was the local hospital, a building that looked the mirror image of Michael's so-called school.

While viewing the Chinese boy's cute masculine face through my wide-spectrum monocular, I'd puzzled for weeks on how best to communicate. He looked my way. My face burned. I crouched lower and adjusted my uncomfortable bra beneath my dreadful, school-approved bleached blouse. After weeks of wanting him to notice me, I now tried to act invisible. After all, I'd never seen a boy from closer than this.

What the heck. I flipped on a portable flash generator I'd discovered while checking out caves by the river and tuned it to an ultraviolet frequency. The dark-haired boy and I had been playing at something for weeks now. "Where are you from?" I whispered. "What happened to your parents? Do you read?"

Most boys didn't I'd been told. "Do you like sports, music?" Not that Union censors allowed much to choose from. I had to settle for playing a game of shadows and light with a boy I'd only seen from across the street behind thick coils of concertina wire.

I flicked my beam three times and waited.

In the rising heat of the afternoon sun, the tacky tar on my school's roof began to ooze. I rose a bit, so it wouldn't stick to my regulation navy blue skorts. In the street below, a parade of electric buses shot past the hospital and scattered a cluster of commuting bicyclists.

A lone mechanized cop enclosed in dull-black shielding paced the exterior of the boy's school. I couldn't imagine anyone fool enough to believe the school was anything but a prison with all the security, barred windows, and wire. My classmates were too paranoid or indifferent to talk about it. My mom swore me never to speak of it.

The mech cop checked the side of the building, glanced along the street, and ambled toward the other corner. I'd watched the hulking mechanical beasts outrun a bus to catch perps, mostly escaped boys. This one appeared bored walking the institute's perimeter. Up on the roof the Chinese boy acted as if he had all the time in the world. After all, if he couldn't leave, what else could he do?

For months I'd watched Michael's School from this roof and from the office of Harmony Director Hanna Surroc, my Cabbage-faced Civics teacher. In all that time, I'd never seen any boys come out. They only went in. Every day the Union scooped up more boys from hiding places all over Knoxville and brought them to school-institutions like this.

A forest green armored bus parked out front to deliver another hapless soul. It tugged at my heart to watch, yet I forced myself to bear witness. Where did they put all the boys?

A violet light flashed from across the way. Then two more. *Not bad.* He got my message and responded one notch down on the light spectrum. *Now what?*

There was much I want to know: how he got there, what it was like inside, what he dreamed of. I tuned my beam and send three flashes of green. Sweat trickled down my neck and not from the steamy heat that beat down on another cloudless day. The tar felt gooey under my knees. I should go before old Cabbage-face caught me again.

I spotted three faint yellow flashes from the boy's roof, hard to see without my monocular. I returned three faded orange bursts and waited.

Our school buzzer sounded. I was late for Surroc's junior Civics class. It would be the third time this month, and never for a better reason than I was sick of lectures about the Second Civil War and how great things have been since. I was due for more detention time. Harmony Director Surroc was convinced she could "reform" and "conform" me.

Can't wait!

On the curb before the boy's school, a tall redhead with a scruffy beard emerged from the bus. They'd bound his hands tight behind him. His muscles bulged. He wore a maroon tracking collar like my Chinese friend and chains around his ankles that forced him to take small steps toward the building. Like all the boys who arrived here, the redhead looked back before he entered the darkened glass doorway, a final glance at freedom. His sweet, frightened eyes called out to me. Then he was gone.

Looking up, I almost missed three red flashes from across the street. "Okay, let's see how clever you are." I tuned my beam to infrared and aimed three bursts to the Chinese boy. In the image through my monocular, he held something to his eye. I couldn't be sure if it was like mine.

Something rustled nearby.

I scooted behind one of the air conditioning units, hoping it wasn't Cabbage-faced Surroc or one of her snitches out looking for me. I expected the Chinese boy to beam back red, asking for a message in the visible range. He surprised me with three infrared bursts. Now that we were both signaling beyond the capability of the unaided eye, what did I want to say, and would he understand?

I'd taught myself Morse code since I couldn't think of anything else he might know. When I'd researched the subject, I came across flag signals, but that was asking for serious trouble. *Hello*, I send.

U have company, he sent back. *Short brown hair.*

It took a moment for the content of his message to register.

4

Someone brushed my arm. "Belle, I knew I'd find you here." It was my adopted sister, Janine, a year younger. I was the adopted one, and she wasn't to know.

"Babe, you can't be late for class."

She grabbed my monocular and scanned buildings across the street: the hospital and the institute. "Surroc is looking for you."

I didn't see the boy and prayed Janine didn't, either.

The door to the roof squealed as someone threw it open. "I know you're up here," old Cabbage-face said.

I wanted to strangle Janine for putting herself at risk for me, again, but I couldn't. "Stay here. I distract her. Then get your fanny back to class."

"Don't do anything crazy," she said. She knew me too well.

I kissed her forehead and ran across the edge of the roof. Tacky tar grabbed at my flats.

Surroc scooted back toward the steel access door to block my escape. "There's nowhere to go."

Old Cabbage-face was so predictable. I sprinted in those miserable flats, praying the tar didn't tear off their flimsy soles. As I headed down one wing of the school, I glanced back to see Surroc in a panic to stop me from reaching the door at the other end.

She wasn't quick enough, but the door was locked.

"Don't make me put a collar on you," Surroc said.

That sent shudders up my spine. Criminals, boys, and those who breached Tenn-tucky's harmony laws had to wear the stupid metal chokers. Aside from having tracking devices, police remotes could trigger the collars to zap you. It was risky to swim or even take a shower with one on.

"Stop before you ruin your chance to enter the cop intern program," Surroc yelled.

That would almost make running worthwhile, though the alternative could be worse: environmental cleanup.

Glancing back, I saw Janine's worried face. *Get moving.* She disappeared into the stairwell while Cabbage-face focused on me. Now that I'd protected my baby sister, I considered what to do.

Surroc stood with her hands on her chubby hips.

You've got me.

TWO

I reached the end of the main-building's roof and the drop to the auditorium below. I jumped. Disappearing from Surroc's view, I landed on all fours on another tarred surface, thankfully in the shade. I ran to the edge of the auditorium, counted my blessings that there was no concertina wire, and glided down the auditorium's drainpipe.

After I reached concrete, I sprinted along the side of the auditorium. Adrenalin kicked in as in cross-country. A bus almost sideswiped me. I jumped back into a mob of sweaty bicyclists. *Sorry.*

They scattered and rang their squeaky bells.

Before the next bus came, I sprinted down a side-street. *Never look back,* my cross-country coach had taught me. Of course she also taught there were no winners or losers, only harmony.

Right.

Along the sidewalk, women dressed in bland harmony-approved pastels scattered out of my way and stared with in-bred suspicion. I must be a criminal to run, to be out-of-place in town when I should be in school. Several used wrist phones to call it in, tying up emergency lines.

I turned the corner and slowed to a fast walk, hoping to blend in. Not likely with my school-approved pale blouse and blue skorts. I smiled at all the wary faces, nodded, and said hello.

Until I first became interested in the black-haired boy with almond eyes, I never thought how strange this might seem to our ancestors. I didn't see a single male on the streets, on bicycles, or in buses. Never had. While mention of such in school got you detention or worse, Mom often talked to me about life before the Second Civil War, before the Federal Union defeated Outland rebels and chose to make the Union all-female.

How did they do this? Union mech warriors overwhelmed the rebels, crushing them within weeks. Some said it was the hand of God, or Goddess, depending on your beliefs. Oh, you meant the fertility bit. Labs used EggFusion to fuse eggs from two women to create new life. You couldn't get pregnant unless you wanted to. Even then, you had to wait years for Federal approval for up to two daughters, and hope the process worked.

My thoughts returned to the Chinese boy with his charming smile. Well, one time I'd seen him smile. Most times he carried a focused scowl. I wouldn't smile either if they cooped me up in a boarding school. Instead, I was stuck in an all-girls school with Cabbage-faced Surroc and her harmony rules. My joy came from watching her squirm.

There was something about connecting with a forbidden boy that appealed to me. Anything outlawed by our dear Union: energetic music, movies without harmony morals, and books Mom kept in her private library that could get her arrested. I liked anything that didn't smack of enforced harmony with officials telling me what I was allowed to do, think, and feel. Because if I did, thought, or felt something of my own, I was not being harmonious.

Bull.

Legs pumping, I turned another corner and almost

tripped when roof-tar on my flimsy flats stuck to the sidewalk like tacky tape. I passed dozens more cams that could trace my movements.

Yeah, I'm acting stupid. At least I'm free.

I imagined myself as the Chinese boy escaping from the school-prison, breaking for freedom. I got this from the look on Red's face before they sucked him inside the institution. Maybe they weren't that different from me.

The next street swarmed with large black insects: women cops in tarnished-black mechanical exoskeletons that gave them bus-speed mobility and brute force to contain any threat, even the most brutish of men. I'd never seen any except on security vids the school fed Janine and me to entice us to sign up for security careers.

Not on your life.

I turned and sprinted away from the boy's school. I expected old Cabbage-face to pop out at each street crossing. She wasn't fast enough, but that didn't help. I was running in circles, postponing the inevitable.

Breathe. Savor the moment.

In the past, Surroc would have caught me already. Some said I was pushing for attention or testing our security. They were wrong. Though I hated school, I loved to learn.

When she'd caught me before, old Cabbage-face made me sit in her office, where I could watch the prison-school. When I didn't show the proper humility, she put me in solitary for an hour: the broom closet. There I was alone with my thoughts.

The swarm of mech cops meant someone had escaped from Michael's. Was it my Chinese friend, the redhead in shackles, or someone else I might have seen? This excited my blood to keep running.

If I were a boy, I'd cross the river into forested hills. But the river was too wide to swim and Union mech patrols monitored every bridge. There might be a safe-house nearby, a traitor who harbored boys. But who would risk helping an escaped boy given the penalty of prison or worse?

My eyes searched for clues of the boys. Part of me was excited. Yet I was also terrified, the result of too many harmony tales of the dangers boys presented. As I ran, women kept their distance. Bicyclists crossed to the other side of the street. Shopkeepers closed doors to Federal Clothiers, Federal Hardware, Tenn-tucky Bistro, forewarned no doubt by e-cast to be on the lookout for boys or for me. Surely I wasn't that important.

While in great shape, my legs rebelled from tension, and not having clear goals. I turned the next corner, past a Union Burgers & Subs. A boy with dark hair tore off down an alley before I could see if it was my Chinese friend, too short for Red. I was impressed he made it this far and felt propelled to chase after him.

One of the huge black insects cut me off and sprinted after the boy, focused on her prey. No doubt the cop inside radioed my location. I doubled back and reached the next corner, Tenn-tucky Clothiers. Three more mech cops entered the street. Cams and cops surrounded me.

My e-com vibrated. I ducked into a Union Burgers & Subs to catch my breath. Two mech cops sprinted by. My e-com flashed: Surroc. That meant she was back in her office to look up my number. *Focus on me, not Janine, you fat cabbage-head.*

I squirted myself a cup of water and ducked into the restroom. It was a lousy hiding place. I hoped they didn't have cams. The thought gave me the creeps. Too many voyeurs got their kicks watching us common folk. I knew it was a stretch to think of myself as ordinary when my adoptive Mom was a state senator. Yet she was an outcast herself, in the dreaded opposition, nothing to be envied.

When my e-com vibrated again, I almost turned it off. It was Mom so I picked up.

"What in the world?" she began and fell silent.

Guilt enveloped me. Another stupid prank. More black

marks on my permanent record. My entire future disintegrated before me. I didn't have the heart to tell her our precious Janine almost got caught. Even that was my fault.

"I'm sorry, Mom. I hate school and all the ..." I wanted to say lies, but caught myself. The Union monitored all frequencies. I didn't need them questioning Mom. She was already in enough hot-water with the governor and Tenn-tucky's Police Chief.

"Get back to school," Mom said. "Take whatever punishment they give with grace."

"Yes, ma'am."

"Don't sass me."

"No, ma'am." *Please don't un-adopt me.*

* * *

I headed out to what had become deserted streets. People hid when mech cops appeared.

Seeing a black-demon mech cop run down the street got me wondering if the boy was still free.

Hugging the storefront of Federal Office Supply, I inched my way back toward school. I was in no hurry either to run into mech cops or to face Surroc. Halfway down the block, I spotted non-mech uniformed cops surrounding Michael's School. I backed into an alley to conceal myself and waited for my opportunity to cross.

Someone grabbed my wrists. "Got you, you little street urchin."

I wrenched free before she could tag me, and moved toward the street. Cops lined the sidewalk. No escape. I turned and studied my cop's face: weathered, tough, no nonsense, not a lump of buttered cabbage like Surroc. The cop held a taser aimed at my neck and fired.

Awaiting the jolt, I froze. Muscles twitched in anticipation of paralysis to come. I fell back against a stone wall and braced myself, though that didn't help. The worst part was losing control and peeing your pants, the ultimate humiliation. I whimpered, hating myself for acting so weak. She had me; yet she didn't trigger the juice.

I hung my head and acted submissive to let her know I wouldn't resist. Surroc was one thing. Cop-trouble was far worse, particularly since becoming a cop was the best I could hope for, according to my Harmony Director. In any case, I didn't want to add assaulting a cop to my list of offenses. "Please, I'll return to school. Promise."

I looked behind the tough cop to see her partner, a big-boned brunette. She adjusted the maroon collar on the boy I'd seen earlier. It wasn't my Chinese friend or Red. This one was smaller, round eyes, sandy blonde hair, and looked ready to pee himself if he hadn't already.

If he's dangerous, I'm a giraffe.

The big-boned cop pushed the boy toward the street, his arms cuffed behind him. She even chained his legs so he couldn't run. Like he could get far with that collar. Cops would have had him in convulsions before he got ten feet.

"Take him in," the tough cop said. "I'll handle this one."

THREE

While the big cop led the boy out of sight, I hung my head and leaned against the stone wall. "I know truancy is a serious offence. I won't do this again. Seeing that boy scared sense into me," I wanted to help the boy. He reminded me of protecting Janine.

"You're not half as scared of the boy as you should be," the cop said. She removed the taser contacts from my neck. "You've been shocked before. Haven't you?"

"Yes, ma'am." Twice, which was one reason I didn't run. Getting shocked while running could lead to serious injuries.

"Annabelle Scott, isn't it?" The cop checked her wrist-com. "I'm Lieutenant Brooks. You're mother is a state senator."

I nodded. My blood was ready to boil. I didn't like people bringing up Mom, as if my sins had anything to do with her. I turned to run. The cop hadn't reloaded her taser. She'd have to outrun me or use her regular gun.

Before I could make my move, she slammed me against the wall of the retail store. "You're full of piss, aren't you?"

I'd never heard an adult use such language. My face burned. Her fist stung against my shoulder. She had power

I hadn't anticipated from someone not wearing a mech suit.

"I'm a nobody who skipped school," I said, eyeing the street for an escape.

"I doubt that." She stepped back to reload the taser. "Someone signaled the boy's school. I suspect you. I always get to the facts, so don't bullshit me."

"No, ma'am." I was used to predictable Surroc, not this. "I want to return to school."

"What's your hurry? I'm not done with you."

Feeling trapped got me thinking about jail: torn from Mom and Janine. Plus all the shame I'd bring to my family for breaching harmony. My eyes fill with sissy tears.

"You romanticize being some modern-day Juliette, don't you? This isn't a game."

Really? Seems like one. Who is Juliette?

"Someone helped these boys escape. If I find it's you, I'll send you away for a long time."

I couldn't see how I'd helped anyone escape, except by distracting the cops. She'd said boys, plural, though. Did the Chinese boy make it? What about Red?

Scanning the narrow alleyway, my mind flooded with ideas: distract cops, give boys directions. What else could I do? Then I imagined Janine, tearing herself apart because she couldn't prevent me doing something stupid.

"Why would I help boys when they're all brutes?" I asked to keep Brooks busy.

"Spare me your class regurgitations. You think you're one tough chick, don't you?"

A pathetic one right now.

She studied her wrist-com, and then looked at me. "I see you're security-tracked, which means you know better. I should haul your ass to jail. Your mom might get you out in a week or so, but that would cost her. I don't think you want that."

"Please. I promise to be good."

"You don't get it, kiddo. Helping boys is a federal offense, serious jail time."

I stared into her tough face. I was quaking inside. Then I reached a moment of clarity. "You have other plans for me, don't you?"

Brooks grinned. "I believe you have what it takes to be a cop if you lose that chip on your shoulder."

"So you're offering me jail or become a cop?"

"Cop internship, actually. It would focus your energy. I'd be willing to sponsor you in the hope of turning you around. Two afternoons a week at first. Then we'll see."

"What about child labor laws? At fifteen, shouldn't I be out having fun, instead of working my butt off?"

Brooks narrowed her eyes. "State deems you're old enough for the intern program. I should think that's preferable to the alternative."

"There you are." A plump cop with captain stripes approached. Captain Barb Voss looked bigger in person than in our school security vids. "Lieutenant Scarlatti said I'd find you here. Ah, you caught our little troublemaker."

I held my tongue and mulled over Brooks' offer. I didn't want to become a cop, enforcing rules over what people could say and do, and imprisoning boys. However, helping boys was a serious offense. As a minor I might get two weeks, maybe a month. Then I'd be out and no longer tied down with expectations of cop internship. Unfortunately, being security tracked meant that my future was limited. Cop was my best option.

The rotund captain sneered at me. "Why expect better from the daughter than from her obnoxious mother? You're all trash. I've got a jail cell for you."

Brooks pushed me aside before I could defend my family. "Captain, I'd like to bring this grunt into the intern program. She's security-tracked. Why waste a valuable resource?"

Voss was another reason not to become an intern. I'd

have to deal with her hatred for Mom, which was all over the news.

The captain glared at me, then at Brooks. "You sure you want to put your entire career on the line for this trash?"

"Let's not judge her based on her mom. I think we can turn this one around."

I stepped back into the alley's shadows wishing I could become invisible. I didn't want jail. I needed Janine around to quell this anger before I did something even more stupid.

While Brooks argued with Voss I heard my sister in my head, where she'd taken root years ago. After all, she was the smart one, studying a year ahead of her grade to challenge me to pass my classes. She would say, "Internship provides job security," as if I cared, "and gets us out of school two afternoons a week."

Most important, I didn't want Janine to follow my example. She would. I was such a bad influence on her. Yet she was so sweet back at me. I couldn't hurt Mom and by association put a black mark on Janine's record. I looked at Brooks and Voss arguing. I'd never had anyone except Mom stand up for me before and Brooks knew nothing about me.

"She's a lost cause," Captain Voss said. Her rotund figure reminded me of a cow, a fat cow-face.

I'm not a lost cause. I'll prove it.

My gut screamed to say no to the cop internship. But once I did jail time, they'd watch me more closely and tag me with a parole collar for all to see. However stifled I felt already would get much worse. On the other hand, I could take up Brooks' challenge and find a way to stick it to Voss.

"I'd be honored to take the challenge of becoming a good cop intern," I said.

Voss stopped and squinted at me, as if she could zap me with her mind.

Inwardly, I smiled. After all, if I became a cop intern, Surroc wouldn't be able to inflict her little punishments on me.

Brooks shook my hand. "You won't regret it."

We'll see. I smiled.

Voss screwed up that cow-face of hers and glared as if she could stab my eyeballs. I'd welcome that to escape her spiteful image.

"One step out of line and I'll nail you and your entire family," she said. "Don't think I won't."

I didn't for a moment doubt she'd try. I held my facial muscles taut as a statue to deny her any reaction. It was something I'd had considerable practice with at school.

Captain Voss spit on the sidewalk, something that would have gotten me arrested for disharmony. She strutted away with her look of disgust.

I focused on the retreating cow, swishing her tail with her awkward waddle. Brooks slapped a wrist-com like hers onto my left wrist. I pull away, but she held firm.

"This links you into our com-net so we can contact each other at any time."

"And so you can track my movements," I added. It almost felt like that boy's maroon collar.

Brooks nodded. "If you get into trouble, all you have to do is push these two contacts." She pointed to opposite sides of the wrist-com. "That brings help."

Just what I needed, a way to have cops on my backside.

"Don't trigger this accidently or as a prank. You don't want to know what hell can descend on you."

I had a pretty good imagination, enhanced by prior close encounters of the wrong kind.

"Shall I report to the cop station tomorrow?" I asked in the hope of getting away before things got worse.

The deserted street came back to life as cops faded away.

"You start now," Brooks said. "One of the boys still eludes us. We believe someone helped him. Heaven can't help if that was you, but I'm offering you a way to redeem yourself."

Stunned, I stared at Brooks; then lowered my eyes. "Why me?"

"We picked up your signal. You may not have helped the Chinese boy escape, but you were in contact with him."

I closed my eyes. *Dumb. Dumb. Dumb!*

My breath caught. He could still be free.

Brooks' eyes narrowed, studying me. My marble façade crumbled. I was betraying myself, but I recovered. "Okay, so I've seen boys across from my school. If the Union doesn't want me seeing them, why locate them so close. Why not send them to the country?"

"You're a clever girl. You tell me."

Not used to this type of interrogation, I hesitated. "They couldn't find a better use for a closed mental hospital?"

Brooks nodded. "Sounds about right. Help me find him. In return, I'll sponsor you into the intern program. That'll keep your sorry ass out of jail, for your benefit and for your family."

I felt myself on a very short leash. Not seeing any alternative, I nodded. "What do you want me to do?"

"Follow me." Brooks led the way back toward school. "As an intern, you need to learn to follow orders. Can you do that?"

Do I look like someone who follows orders? "Yes, ma'am."

She studied me and kept moving. "Anything you think of that might help me catch the boy you're to tell me. Is that understood?"

"Yes, ma'am." I struggled to keep up with her cop boots. My tacky flats kept sticking to concrete like chewing gum. "Why don't we track his collar?"

"Now, why didn't I think of that? He masked the transmitter."

Clever. I tried not to show my reaction, though I got the

impression Brooks could see through me. "I don't see how I can help."

Brooks grinned. "Because, you little urchin, you play hide and seek with your school, and with cops. Think. Where would you go?"

Scanning stores, restaurants, and Union-run apartment buildings, I considered where I'd go to escape ever-present cams and infrared sensors. But I didn't want her catching my friend. "Isn't an intern supposed to get some kind of brainwashing?"

"It's called indoctrination. For now, we'll keep this simple. You're not to act on your own. You'll shadow and watch me. You'll advise me with any thoughts no matter how bizarre that might lead to this boy."

A snitch in other words. I felt as if I were betraying my own sister. "Do I get a weapon to protect against this brute?"

"No, so stay close."

I noticed how respectful pedestrians were when Brooks passed, nodding and smiling. It made me wonder whether they had secret thoughts that they hid behind their facial masks.

We reached my school with the auditorium to my right and administrative offices to the left. "I don't think a boy would come here." At least I hoped not. Having them near Janine gave me chills.

Harmony Director Surroc greeted us on the front steps, her cabbage-face beaming. "Thanks for returning our runaway, officer. Sorry for whatever trouble she caused." Her bright-white teeth grinned with delight. I could almost see the slow churn of her brain thinking up new punishments for me.

Standing on the bottom step, I adopted a zoned-out face. After all, if I was going to be a dumb blonde, might as well look the part.

Brooks met old Cabbage-face halfway and shook her hand. "Afraid we have police business. We need her help."

Surroc looked stunned, which stretched a grin onto my face. Cop internship might be tolerable if it got old Cabbage-face twisted in knots.

"I don't understand," Surroc said. "She skipped school. Truancy is—"

"Annabelle is helping with an investigation as a test for entry into the intern program."

"Oh? She hasn't … I mean she's been … we can't allow this."

"Need I remind you that police business takes precedence over school matters?"

"No," Surroc muttered. "But she's incapable of following rules. She'll make a poor cop." That sounded strange coming from someone who dangled cop as the carrot to get me to behave.

"I take full responsibility," Brooks said. "Thanks for your cooperation." She nudged me to follow her.

After we crossed the street, she stopped me. "We have our work cut out if you're to become a cop."

"Yes, ma'am, but Surroc—"

"Is a pompous ass. Still, you have to get past that if you're to survive in this world. You'll run into others like her."

"You mean Captain Voss?" I said.

"I didn't say that."

"Then you agree."

Brooks pushed me against a Tenn-tucky Electronics storefront. "Don't mess with me. Don't mistake my offer as weakness."

Rubbing my sore shoulder, I wanted to hate Brooks for being one of the thugs hunting down my friend, but she was a puzzle. I felt like an alien plopped into some foreign world where all the rules had changed. I'd learned to deal with old Cabbage-face. Brooks seemed one step ahead of me.

All I knew was I didn't want to go to jail. "Now what?"

FOUR

Brooks checked her wrist-com and frowned. "Think, Annabelle. If you were on the run, where would you go?"

Trap! Don't give up your hiding places.

My mind spun. Could she read my thoughts? Was I that transparent? It made me wonder if I'd been kidding myself that I've gotten away with white lies at home and dark ones with Surroc.

"As a girl, I'd find a friendly place; find someone to talk to. If I distracted her long enough, she might agree to help before she became suspicious and turned me in."

"For this exercise you're a boy."

"I've never considered it from their perspective." A lie.

"Look, I know you're only here as an alternative to jail. This is important. Think of the implications if this boy gets away."

He could find his family and have a life.

"You don't seem convinced," Brooks said, nudging me along. "If he gets away, he could help rebels. He could assault girls at your school, even your sister."

Janine!

I couldn't breathe. I didn't want to believe that's what he wanted.

I calmed myself as I did when old Cabbage-face interrogated me. If I were an imprisoned boy, I'd want freedom, not to go around hurting people.

"What if he's not a brute?" I asked. "What if he just misses his family? Surely you don't believe taking his family away is right." I shut up before I said too much, before Brooks arrested me for disharmony.

Brooks hesitated. "That's a decision for the Judicial Board, young lady. Our job is to stop boys running around with their collars masked so we can't find them."

"If he walked down Main Street in an orange outfit, with his neck puffy to hide his tracking collar on a steamy day like this, don't you think people would report him?"

"Where were you when I got this assignment?" Brooks asked with a scowl. "Of course he's not walking the streets like that. He must have had help to mask the device and change clothes."

"Who would help him?"

"Underground Railroad," she said.

"That's a myth." I'd read about this group during the first Civil War, though the Federal Union denied the existence of an Underground Railroad today. It would imply there were boys who needed saving.

"It's not a myth. Let's start with the institute." Brooks headed toward Michael's School. "Assume you're inside the school and you want out. How do you go?" She glared at me as if I would know. After all, I'd just escaped my school.

"I'd have to see inside the school to figure that out."

"Okay, but no tricks."

"Are you kidding? We're going inside?" My throat closed. Brooks kept surprising me. Or she was trying to trick me.

While picking up her pace, Brooks sent a message on her wrist-com.

Avoiding a few bicyclers, we crossed the street in front

of the hospital and turned toward the school. On the other side of the street, old Cabbage-face stood on the steps of my school. I almost felt sorry for her. Brooks had removed her daily joy. I grinned.

"How can the boy mask the tracking device in the collar?" I asked.

Brooks stopped. "Are you messing with me?"

"No, ma'am. If I'm to help, I need to know what he does."

She nodded, though I saw doubt. "Aluminum seems to block the signal." She resumed walking.

"Aluminum foil? It can't be that simple." I studied the large windows of the hospital and the barred ones of the boys' school next door for any hint of my friend.

"Double-wrapped, yes."

"What about infrared. Doesn't the school have sensors? Can't we scan buildings and count people."

"Their scanners can't confirm male," Brooks said.

"He found a way to mask infrared?"

"Remind me not to underestimate you."

I felt as if I'd given away one of my secrets.

"There are ways," Brooks said, "but quite complicated."

"Nano-fabrics?"

"Polymer blends. It would require help on the outside."

I wanted more details, though not at the risk of turning Brooks against me. Aluminum foil I'd remember. It might help with my student ID and travel fob so I could escape old Cabbage-face.

As we headed toward the boys' school, three black-shielded mech cops circled the grounds. I would have loved to see their puzzled faces. All this technology to catch a single boy and he was winning. Got to love him for that.

Regular uniformed cops mulled around outside the large concrete hospital to my left. No way would I want to be stuck in there. An ambulance pulled up the drive. Someone could have helped the boy that way. I kept that to myself.

As we passed the hospital, I stared down the narrow alley that separated it from the school. I spotted hundreds of cams and sensor boxes covering the area. The boy would be crazy to cross here.

Brooks studied me. "I see wheels turning. Spill. Tell me what you're seeing and thinking."

"If he crossed this alley, you'd have him in custody."

"And?"

Or he'd be in the hospital, where I wouldn't go. Too many people and cams. "There are no windows or doors leading out this side of the school."

"You're not convinced."

"What are your cams telling you?"

Brooks continued toward the institute entrance. "Cams tracked three boys down this alley. We caught all three."

"And the boy you found."

Brooks frowned. "He left out the back. We've caught all four who showed up on cams. The Chinese boy you were watching never did."

"So he's still in the school."

We reached the Michael's School entrance, the one I'd watched earlier from the roof of my school. The windows were black. A grandmotherly woman wearing an administrator's suit like Surroc greeted us with a scowl. She moved with more determination than I first expected. "We've searched the entire school. Everything's in lockdown. You won't find him here."

"We'd like to look around," Brooks said while shaking the woman's hand.

I wanted to ask how the administrator knew for sure that he wasn't in the building. I held my tongue as she led us inside what felt like a dungeon. The entryway was dark except for light from the street until the blackened doors closed, robbing us of the last flicker of daylight. A blast of cold air caused me to shiver after the sticky outside heat.

Someone was watching. I felt violated in the dark with sensors picking up more than my infrared signature: probably chemicals, heart rate, and a full body scan. After a few moments, another set of doors opened. Lobby lights bathed us. An officious woman sat behind a metallic desk. She studied an array of screens, no doubt reading scan tests on me or watching hundreds of cams and sensors from all around the school.

If this hadn't been my idea, I would have turned back. "Any way he could have jumped off the roof and bypassed cams?"

The administrator studied me. She looked much younger than I'd thought, though she would benefit from a more colorful wardrobe. "Overlapping cams cover every inch of the grounds. Infrared sensors aimed in and out would have picked up any signature as it did for the four boys you've caught."

I was surprised she talked so openly in front of me. Adults other than Mom rarely did. The administrator must have assumed I was already an intern. Brooks nodded for me to continue.

"When did you lose their collar signals?"

"Before they crawled under the wall."

"A tunnel?"

"A gap they enlarged. We've since sealed it. We've examined every inch of the school perimeter and closed off similar escape risks."

I was enjoying this challenge. Thinking of escapes connected me to stories of my father escaping when I was three, though they caught and executed him. Keeping Brooks and the school administrator busy might help my friend.

"What about jumping off the roof?" I asked.

"A parachute we would have detected."

I was stumped and impressed. "No closet he could be hiding in?"

The woman shook her head.

I was torn between figuring out the puzzle so I could meet the boy, and not wanting him caught. I wandered toward huge steel doors on the hospital side of the school. Security was tight. I reminded myself that I'd never seen any boys coming out of this institution.

The unnamed administrator—she didn't offer and wasn't wearing a nametag—unlocked the doors. She led us down a high-ceiling concrete corridor with dingy beige walls, smelling of sweat and ammonia. I sneezed. Rows of steel doors lined the hallway.

"Are these classrooms?" I asked, going with the school-titled name of this place.

"Boys aren't like girls," the administrator said. "You have to keep them separated or they cause trouble. We've triple checked each room. There are no boys here and no possible escapes."

She didn't offer to show me inside. This time Brooks glared at me not to push it. I sulked down a corridor that resembled a dark medieval dungeon, the jail cell that cow-faced Voss had for me. These were so unlike my classrooms it made me wonder what I'd been griping about. Surroc was a declawed pussy cat by comparison.

My stomach did somersaults. I stifled a sneeze. It made no sense to come here if we couldn't ask questions and inspect these rooms. I already knew the answer. The Chinese boy didn't escape this way and there were things the administrator didn't want me to see: torture chambers, beatings, bloody experiments. I tried to shut off my imagination.

Brooks shook me. We were back in the lobby. The tour was over. I was relieved and disturbed.

"Do you have a basement?" I asked.

The administrator scowled. This time Brooks stared at the woman.

"That's how the boys escaped," the administrator admitted. "They found crumbled concrete and dug their way out. This is why we keep boys isolated."

"Can we see?" I asked.

"More of what you've seen, only underground."

"Humor us," Brooks said. She winked my way when the administrator led us toward elevators across the lobby.

I didn't want to be friends with Brooks. She was working me to get my guard down. But I didn't like the alternative. I imagined myself in this place with no windows and no escape. Did Brooks bring me to scare me into helping? It was working.

The woman took us down to the real dungeon. As soon as we got off the elevator, the dank odor made me sneeze and cough. I wouldn't be any good escaping from a place like this.

Lights were dim. The concrete floor carried dark stains. I told myself it was only my imagination. "What's the difference between these rooms and the ones upstairs?" I asked. Cam boxes poked out of the ceiling every ten feet."

"Those are classrooms and meeting rooms. These are for boys who misbehave."

"Any boys escape from …" I stopped before I said "cells."

"No boys escaped from solitary," the administrator said. "The walls are foot-thick steel and nano-polymer reinforced concrete. Even if a boy found a hammer and chisel, which they can't, it would take him longer than we hold him here to break out. We inspect these rooms daily. The four we caught escaped from a break in the tunnel in back using a sonic excavator someone smuggled in. We've reinforced that break and two others. We've also installed sensors to detect sonic equipment."

I wasn't convinced. "How many rooms do you have down here?"

"Sixty-four."

"How many are in use right now?"

"That isn't relevant," the woman said. "I already told you no one has escaped from solitary."

My heart tightened at the thought of so many boys in solitary, or even one, my friend. "I was hoping to see one."

"Lieutenant Brooks, is this necessary?"

"Humor us," Brooks said. "After all, you don't know how the other boy escaped."

The administrator took us to the end of a long yellowing corridor and unlocked a thick steel door. When she opened it, the smell was overpowering of feces and urine. I gagged yet forced myself to enter the dark room.

A yellowed light came on with dim illumination to confirm the horror. Straw covered the concrete floor that measured seven feet on a side with no sink or toilet. There was no sign of human waste, though the stench lingered. Along the hospital side, scratches marred the wall as if someone had tried to dig their way out of this hell-hole, a feeble attempt, probably with bloodied fingernails.

"You've checked all these rooms for any sign that someone dug their way out?" I asked. I held my breath and left the room.

"Thoroughly," the administrator said. "I told you it would be unpleasant. Boys are pigs. Good thing we've banned both."

Stepping across the corridor to escape the stench, I glimpsed a side hallway. "Where does that lead? To the hospital?"

"When we have emergencies, we prefer not to parade boys along the street. These doors are secure on both ends. I assure you the boy couldn't waltz out that way without a lot of help."

I smiled. The last place I'd want to land is a busy hospital. I didn't want to think how injured a boy would be before they'd move him.

I couldn't get out of Michael's Prison fast enough. When we reached steamy fresh air, I ran to the street and stopped at the sight of my school across the way. I couldn't rid myself of the foul odor of the prison basement.

UNINTENDED REBEL

Brooks held my arm to steady me. "Sorry about that. You insisted. Now what aren't you telling me?"

I looked up. "How can we treat boys like that?"

She looked around. "Watch your tongue. There are ears everywhere."

"I don't care."

Brooks shoved me along the sidewalk. "One more word and I'll arrest you. Now, unless you want me to back out of our deal, tell me how the boy escaped."

Helping to capture my friend went against everything I believed in. The thought churned my stomach after seeing the conditions at Michael's. I didn't want to betray him, but I couldn't survive jail. It would kill Mom and Janine.

The massive hospital before us from the right angle could have been a cousin to the boys' school. Built around the same time, the institute had served as a mental ward before they turned it into Michael's School for Boys.

"That makes sense." Brooks grabbed my arm and dragged me into the hospital emergency room.

While she talked to a brunette at the nurse's station, I watched a mother and her two little girls. Tears filled my eyes for the brother I would never know, for what I was about to do to the Chinese boy to save myself. Yet, if he was in the hospital, what was he thinking? My only hope was to make this another distraction, another false lead buying him time. To salve my own conscience, I settled on that.

From the emergency room door I watched mech cops surround the hospital. Plain-clothed and uniformed cops entered in droves and fanned out. There must have been fifty, all for a lone boy who had to be petrified. I was.

"Come on," Brooks said. "Let's check out this side of the tunnel for clues."

I followed her down a series of bright-white corridors. I noted similarities to the prison next door, except the hospital had tiled floors, drop ceilings, and brilliant-white paint.

When we turned the corner away from the nano-med wing, a nurse behind the counter caught my eye: tall, muscular, with a handsome Chinese face. He looked cute even dressed like a girl. I smiled and kept moving. I wanted to stop and talk. Then Brooks would arrest us both.

Suddenly, my body turned prickly with hot needles. I was endangering not only myself, but my Mom, barely surviving as a political outsider, and my sister who would endure the worse of my actions. The school and all her friends would ostracize her for our association.

"Did you see something?" Brooks asked, looking around.

"This place is a mirror image of …" I almost said prison, "… school next door."

Around the next corner was an elevator, in the dingiest part of the hospital. Garbage pickup was to the left with a large locked bin for medical waste disposal. I wondered why my Chinese friend hadn't gone out with the trash. But camera boxes lined the exit and around the elevator, inspecting everything that left the hospital. He might have tried this and then scurried looking for another way out. And I brought the cavalry.

I damned my cowardice, my need for self-preservation.

When we reach the basement, Brooks led me to the hospital side of the tunnel connecting with Michael's. The worn and cracked concrete surprised me. This was a well-used passage, either from the mental health days or from the boys. All I had were questions that Brooks wouldn't or couldn't answer.

"As you can see," Brooks said, "the door is locked on this side with sensors monitoring the area. The nurse is checking cam-feeds."

It was only a matter of time before they caught him. "Maybe I was wrong."

"Assume someone helped him."

"Whoever helped could have driven him away. In which case, he's no longer here."

"With so many cams and sensors, his helper might only have gotten him this far. Then what?"

I didn't like this game, but I couldn't stop playing. "Once he got upstairs, he'd be by garbage pickup. If I were him, I'd leave with the garbage, get to a dump site out in the country without cams and sensors, and make a run for it."

Brooks nudged me back toward the elevator. "Clever. We'll check the trucks and dump sites. Wherever he went, he's no longer down here."

Inwardly I smiled, yet kept my face as still as marble. I didn't want to give up my Chinese friend.

Brooks returned me to the emergency entrance and went to talk to that cow-faced Captain Voss. I felt terrible for what my Chinese friend had been through and for my part in bringing cops to the hospital. I hated being unable to play this safer with Brooks watching so closely. The boy had been clever, hiding in plain sight here at the hospital. He could have waited, changing roles until the cops went away and then made his break. But I brought the cops.

A hand grabbed my shoulder. "What are you doing here?" It was Mom, her weathered face tortured with wrinkles. "I told you to return to school. I've looked all over for you."

"I'm sorry."

"Enough nonsense for one day. Get your fanny home right now. Are you trying to ruin your family?"

"No, Mom. Lieutenant Brooks—"

"More trouble? What am I to do with you?"

"Mom!"

"Later."

Behind Mom I saw Brooks with that tall nurse in his ridiculous outfit, much too small for him. The lieutenant had already cuffed the boy whose only real crime had been wanting freedom. She tugged off his bonnet, revealing shoulder-length coal-black hair. When she ripped aluminum foil from the maroon collar around his neck, he offered no resistance. With so many cops, there was no point.

My stomach churned. My mind whirred thinking of any alternative, but it was too late. The boy looked at me with doleful eyes, breaking my heart. He blinked; twitched. Then I realized it was Morse code:

Thnx. UR not like them.

I wished there was more I could do for him. Maybe as a cop intern I could. Then I saw in Mom's eyes. She'd been the one helping my friend.

OTHER STORIES BY LANCE ERLICK

REGINA SHEN: RESILIENCE (Regina Shen book 1)

Outcast Regina Shen is forced by the World Federation to live on the seaward side of barrier walls built to hold back rising seas from abrupt climate change. A hurricane threatens to destroy what's left of her world, tearing Regina from her family.

Global fertility has collapsed. Chief Inspector Joanne Demarco of the notorious Department of Antiquities believes Regina holds the key to avoid extinction. Regina fights to stay alive and avoid capture while hunting for her family. Does she have the resilience to survive?

REGINA SHEN: VIGILANCE (Regina Shen book 2)

Regina Shen is pursued by the notorious Department of Antiquities for her unique DNA. She jumps the Barrier Wall into the Federation to find her kidnapped sister. Stuck on a heavily-guarded closed-university campus in the mountains, she must use her wits to escape and rescue her sister without letting either of two rival Antiquities inspectors capture her.

REGINA SHEN: DEFIANCE (Regina Shen book 3)

Outcast Regina Shen has DNA the Federation believes can reverse a global fertility collapse. Rival Federation agents fight over capturing Regina to gain power amidst turmoil over who will become the new World Premier. Regina has to flee from Virginia through desert and wilderness to Alaska to hunt a treasure big enough to barter for her freedom and that of her sister.

THE REBEL WITHIN (Rebel Series book 1)

Annabelle Scott lives under the iron rule of a female-dominated régime that forces males to fight to the death to train the military elite. When pressed into service as a mechanized warrior to capture escaped boys, Annabelle stays true to herself by helping some escape. Her defiance endangers everyone she loves and thrusts her to a place of impossible life and death decisions.

THE REBEL TRAP (Rebel Series book 2)

Despite being a military recruit, Annabelle Scott rebels against her female-dominated régime by refusing to kill a handsome boy she fancies and helping him escape. Auditory implants and cameras allow her commander to watch her 24-7. Can she help the boy free his brother from a heavily-guarded geek institute without destroying her family or getting killed?

REBELS DIVIDED (Rebel Series book 3)

The first time Geo sees Annabelle, they meet as enemies and she doesn't kill him, which mystifies them both. It's after the 2nd Civil War with the nation divided into an all-female Federal Union and a warlord controlled Outland. The Outland warlord kidnaps Annabelle's sister and kills Geo's pa. Can Annabelle and Geo overcome mutual distrust and work together to rescue her sister and gain justice for his pa's murder? And will their feelings for each other derail or further their goals?

SHE-DEVIL ROCKS (novelette)

Inspired by *Lord of the Flies*.

Bullied as the smallest of thirteen boys in his class, Bradley is on a plane that crashes on a remote island with a bully who is out of control. Bradley meets a mysterious tomboy who shouldn't be there and has to learn to survive on the hostile island, deal with her, and come to terms with the bully.

REGINA SHEN: INTO THE STORM (novelette)

The novelette that launched the Regina Shen series.

Fifteen-year-old Regina Shen is condemned by the World Federation to live on the seaward side of Great Barrier Walls built to hold back rising seas from abrupt climate change. A hurricane threatens to destroy what's left of her world, tearing Regina from her home and family.

REGINA SHEN: SALVAGE (novelette)

Living on the seaward side of barrier walls built to protect against rising seas, the only means of survival for Regina Shen is underwater salvage, which is banned by the World Federation. After a storm takes a friend's family and home, Regina is determined to help by defying the Federation

MAIDEN VOYAGE (novelette)

Security Chief Nina Rekovic keeps the peace on the all-female Maiden's Ark that left Earth five years before. Distress signal says Earth is lost, stranding lunar colonists. Someone sabotages the vital fertility lab. While balancing Returners she sympathizes with, a dictatorial captain, and an estranged lover who betrays her, can Rekovic solve the conspiracy before she's imprisoned or worse?

WATCHING YOU (short story)

At the intersection of pervasive networks and the Patriot Act, we have the ability and some say the obligation to know everything about everyone. Can privacy survive? Can the individual endure?

Harold is a second-class citizen and a low-level worker in a government surveillance system charged with reviewing "criminal activity." He has private thoughts about a woman he's forbidden from approaching. He will not be deterred.

ABOUT THE AUTHOR

Lance Erlick writes science fiction thrillers that appeal to young adult and adult readers. In the Rebel series, he explores the consequences of following conscience for those coming of age. The Regina Shen series takes place after abrupt climate change leads to the Great Collapse and a new society under the World Federation. Lance is also the author of several shorter stories.

Find out more about the author and his work at LanceErlick.com. Go to that website to sign up to receive free story downloads and occasional email newsletters with updates on new releases and other writing developments.